LU & CLANCY
The Carnival Caper

written by **Adrienne Mason**

illustrated by **Pat Cupples**

Kids Can Press

For Margaret — A.M.
To Caspar — P.C.

Kids Can Press acknowledges the financial support of the Ontario Arts Council,
the Canada Council for the Arts and the Government of Canada,
through the BPIDP, for our publishing activity.

Published in Canada by   Published in the U.S. by
Kids Can Press Ltd.   Kids Can Press Ltd.
29 Birch Avenue   2250 Military Road
Toronto, ON M4V 1E2   Tonawanda, NY 14150

www.kidscanpress.com

Edited by Valerie Wyatt and Stacey Roderick
Designed by Julia Naimska
Printed in Hong Kong by Wing King Tong Company Limited

The hardcover edition of this book is smyth sewn casebound.
The paperback edition of this book is limp sewn with a drawn-on cover.

CM 02 0 9 8 7 6 5 4 3 2 1
CM PA 02 0 9 8 7 6 5 4 3 2 1

National Library of Canada Cataloguing in Publication Data

Mason, Adrienne
The carnival caper

(Lu & Clancy)
ISBN 1-55337-027-9 (bound)   ISBN 1-55074-838-6 (pbk.)

I. Cupples, Patricia II. Title. III. Title: The carnival caper. IV. Series.

GV1548.M38 2002   jC813'.54   C2001-901750-2

Kids Can Press is a Nelvana company

Chapter 1

Endless Summer

Clancy lay on the grass and watched some ants march by. A fly buzzed around his nose, but he was too bored to swat it. He was too bored to do anything.

He missed Lu. She had only been away for two weeks, but it felt like the whole summer. Clancy couldn't wait for her to come home.

He scratched his back on the grass and rolled onto his belly. He was drifting off to sleep when he felt a drop of water on his nose — then another and another. "Must be rain." He opened his eyes and squinted into the sun. "But there's not a cloud in sight!"

Just then, a blast of water hit
him right between the eyes.

"Hey, what's going on?"
yelped Clancy. He heard a
familiar giggle coming from
behind an oak tree. Lu was
home! She leaped on Clancy
and the two friends rolled
and tussled on the grass.

Lu and Clancy, dog detectives, were back together!

Clancy grinned from ear to ear. "Let's grab our
bikes and go find Detective Doberman. Maybe he
needs our help to solve a crime or two."

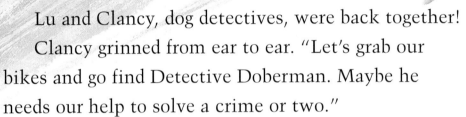

"Can't," said Lu. "My cousin Jake is in town
and I have to take him to the carnival. Why not
come with us?"

"Forget it! I'm not going anywhere with Jake.
All he does is brag about being the world's greatest
magician and do those dumb magic tricks." One time,
Jake had turned Clancy's favorite piggy bank into a
rock and then refused to change it back.

"Come on, Clancy," begged Lu. "We can have
cotton candy and corn dogs."

Clancy folded his arms and shook his head.

Lu tried again. "We can go on the Drop of Doom."

Clancy's ears perked up. The Drop of Doom was the best ride at the carnival. It was their favorite because it was the scariest.

"Well, okay," said Clancy. "We'll be screaming so loud and spinning so fast that Jake won't have a chance to do any magic tricks."

"Drop of Doom, here we come!" yipped the two friends.

Chapter 2

Magic Shmagic

"Magic, shmagic," grumbled Clancy as Jake did yet another trick.

Jake had already pulled an egg out of Lu's ear. Now he was changing a magic potion from green to purple.

"Come on — let's go to the carnival," pleaded Lu.

Jake wasn't listening. He was too busy pouring the purple potion into Clancy's hat.

"Hey! That's my best hat," Clancy barked. But Jake just kept on pouring.

"Don't panic," said Jake. He waved his wand over the hat. "Snickerick, snickeree. Potion, jump into a cup for me." Jake put an empty cup into the hat and waved the wand one more time. Then he pulled out a cup full of potion, took a sip and tossed the hat to Clancy.

Clancy looked into the hat. It was dry! "Hmph," he mumbled. "That was kind of cool."

"Maybe, but it's the last trick I'm going to watch," said Lu. She hopped on her bike and pedaled off. "Let's go!" she shouted over her shoulder. "We don't want to miss the Drop of Doom!"

Clancy rode off after her, but Jake didn't move. "The D-drop of Doom?" he gulped. He wiped the sweat off his brow and slowly, very slowly, got on his bike.

Jake's Hat Trick

This is how Jake poured his magic potion into a hat without getting the hat wet.

You'll need:

• 2 paper cups • scissors • a hat with a flat bottom and tall sides • a cup of water or other liquid

1. Carefully cut out the bottom of one paper cup.

2. Put the other cup (the one with a bottom) in the hat. Pull the sides of the hat up so that you can't see the cup.

3. Now you can do your trick for an audience. Pour the water into the cup in the hat. It will look like you are pouring water into the hat.

4. Say some magic words (snickerick, snickeree), then slip the cup with the cutout bottom inside the cup in the hat. (Don't let your audience see that the bottom is cut out of the cup.)

5. Lift both cups out of the hat and show your audience the dry hat. They will be amazed!

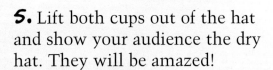

Chapter 3
At the Carnival

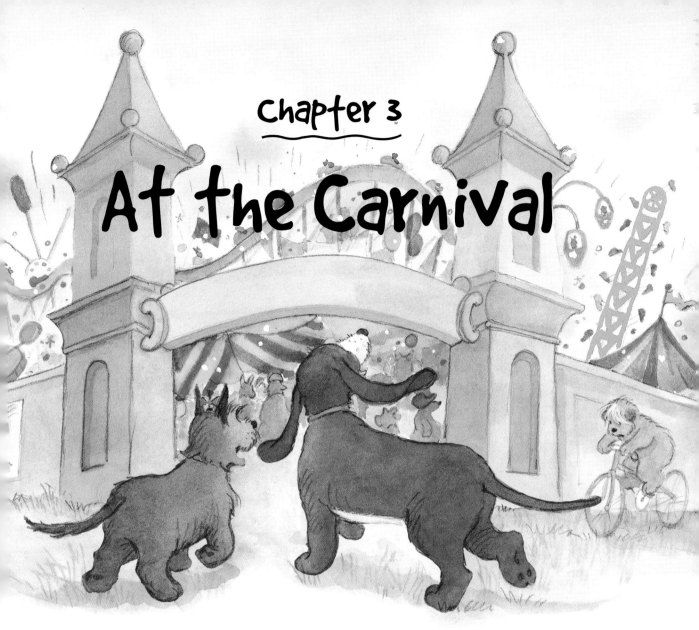

Lu and Clancy drooled at the smell of cotton candy. They could see the Drop of Doom spinning wildly. "Wow! Listen to the screaming," said Clancy. "I can't wait to ride on the Drop of Doom."

Where was Jake? He was taking forever. Finally, he rode slowly around the corner.

"Let's go," yelped Clancy as they bounded through the gates.

"Drop of Doom! Drop of Doom!" chanted Lu.

But Jake wasn't listening. He had wandered off and was staring at a red-and-white striped tent.

"Oh no," groaned Lu. "Jake's found the magic tent."

"This is more like it," said Jake. He waited eagerly for the magic act to begin.

Lu and Clancy squirmed in their seats. Would they *ever* get to ride on the Drop of Doom?

"I should be up on stage," Jake bragged. "I could show that magician a trick or two. Just watch me."

Jake snatched Lu's hair ribbon. He dangled it above her head, then slipped the ribbon through a chocolate bar wrapper. Lu lunged for the ribbon just as Jake snipped through the wrapper and cut it in two.

Now Lu lunged for Jake.

"What's the problem, Lu?" Jake grinned. With a flick of his wrist, he pulled the ribbon out of the wrapper — all in one piece!

Lu fumed. She was getting very tired of Jake. And she didn't want to sit through a magic show. She wanted to ride on the Drop of Doom.

She turned to Clancy to make a plan, but he wasn't listening. He was leaning up against the tent wall, and he had a strange look on his face.

Jake's Magic Ribbon Trick

This is how Jake pretended to cut Lu's ribbon in half. He used a chocolate bar wrapper, but you can do the same trick with an envelope.

You'll need:

- a pair of scissors
- a sealed envelope with both ends cut off
- a ribbon or piece of string

1. Get an adult to help you cut two slits about 3 cm (1 in.) long in the center of the back of the envelope. The slits should be about 1 cm (1/2 in.) apart. This leaves a small "bridge" of paper.

2. Slip the ribbon into one end of the envelope. Thread it over the bridge and through the other end of the envelope as shown.

3. Now you are ready to do your trick for an audience. Hold the envelope up so that they see the front (uncut) side of it.

4. Cut into the envelope, beginning above the bridge. When you come to the bridge, make sure that your scissors are *under* the ribbon so that you don't cut through it. To your audience, it will look as if you have cut the ribbon.

5. Pull out the ribbon. Your audience will be amazed that it is in one piece.

Chapter 4

The Shakedown

Clancy pressed his ear to the wall of the tent. The words "Drop of Doom" caught his attention.

"We'll turn the Drop of Doom into the Drop of Loot," said a gruff voice.

"Mwrah, mwrank," came the answer.

Clancy heard a thwack, then a "Youch!"

"Don't talk with your mouth full, Horace. Stop thinking about your stomach and start thinking about stealing."

"Sorry, Frank." Then there was the loudest belch Clancy had ever heard.

The voices continued. Clancy could hardly believe his ears. Horace and Frank were planning a big shakedown at the Drop of Doom. When the song "Pooches in Paradise" played, Frank would stop the ride so that everyone was upside down. A shower of cameras, purses, jewelry and money would rain down. Then Horace would scurry around and pick up the loot.

We've got to stop them, thought Clancy. He turned to tell Lu, but she and Jake were gone.

Chapter 5
In the Spotlight

Lu and Jake were up on stage, meowing like cats.

"Oh no," groaned Clancy. "The magician has put them into a trance and made them think they're cats."

Clancy watched as the magician had Lu drink a bowl of milk and Jake chase a fuzzy fake mouse. After what seemed like forever, the magician rang a little bell and Lu and Jake were themselves again.

At last, thought Clancy. Now we can get out of here and stop Horace and Frank.

Lu flopped into her seat. Clancy leaned over and told her what he had overheard.

Jake was still up on stage. He wanted to do another trick. Clancy tried to get his attention, but Jake was in the spotlight and he wasn't leaving.

The magician held up a paper bag and dropped in a coin and a ticket for a carnival ride. Then he reached into the bag, removed the ticket and put it in his pocket.

"Now what's in the bag?" he asked Jake.

"That's easy. The coin."

The magician held out the bag. Jake reached in and pulled out … the ticket! The audience laughed. Jake's face went red.

"Do it again," Jake demanded.

20

The magician did the trick again, but Jake still couldn't figure it out.

Lu and Clancy couldn't wait another second. They had to get to the Drop of Doom before Horace and Frank started stealing!

As they raced out of the tent, they heard the magician say to Jake: "For being such a good sport, here is a ticket for a free ride."

Jake looked at the ticket.

His face turned white as a sheet.

GOOD FOR
ONE FREE RIDE
DROP of DOOM

The Magician's Switcheroo Trick

The magician used a ticket for this trick, but you can use any piece of paper that is slightly larger than a coin.

You'll need:

• a paper bag • a coin • 2 identical tickets or small pieces of paper

1. Put one ticket in an empty bag.

2. Now you are ready to perform the trick in front of an audience. Show the audience the coin and the second ticket and put them in the bag.

3. Reach into the bag and hold the coin behind one of the tickets, so that it is hidden. Pull the ticket (with the coin hidden behind it) out of the bag. Don't let your audience see the coin.

4. Choose someone from the audience to reach into the bag. She will think that the coin is still in the bag, but all there will be is the ticket.

Chapter 6
The Culprits

BELCH!

As Lu and Clancy burst out of the magic tent, they were almost run over by a hot dog cart.

"Watch it, kids!" said a gruff-voiced pit bull. His partner, whose mouth was smeared with chocolate, glared at Lu and Clancy, then belched.

A gruff voice and a belch! It had to be Horace and Frank!

"That's them!" Clancy whispered to Lu. "Let's follow them!"

But just as Lu and Clancy were about to follow the two crooks, Jake grabbed them.

Lu struggled. "Let go! We have to get to the Drop of Doom! Now!"

"Sure thing. But first we're going to the Hall of Mirrors." And with that, Jake pushed Lu and Clancy into a dark building.

Jake spent the next hour dragging Lu and Clancy through the carnival.

At the House of Horrors, bats and ghosts jumped out at them, but Lu and Clancy didn't care. They had a crime to stop. They had to get to the Drop of Doom!

Every time Lu and Clancy tried to break away, Jake had another idea. There were stilt walking lessons ...

... a cruise through the Pirate Hall ...

... and even a dance lesson!

Jake dancing? "This is too weird," whispered Lu.

It seemed as if Jake would do anything to avoid the Drop of Doom.

Chapter 7
Card Trick

It was getting late, and Lu and Clancy were still nowhere near the Drop of Doom. How would they ever stop Horace and Frank?

Then Lu had an idea. She turned to Jake. "I bet I know a magic trick that you can't figure out. If I win the bet, we get to go to the Drop of Doom."

"You're on. This will be a snap," said Jake.

Lu ran over to two ladies playing cards at a picnic table. Soon she was back waving an ace of spades and a pair of nail scissors.

"All you have to do is to walk through this playing card." She handed Jake the scissors. "You can use these. Oh, and you have two minutes."

Jake stared at the card and gulped. He snipped a small hole in the middle of the card, but he could only get his big toe through it. He made the hole bigger. His nose fit through, but that was it. Beads of sweat started to form on Jake's forehead. He hemmed and he hawed, but he couldn't figure it out.

"Give up?" asked Lu.

"I guess so," Jake mumbled.

"Here's how to do it." Lu whipped out a new card and grabbed the scissors. With a snip here and a snip there, she made some cuts in the card. In seconds, she and Clancy walked right through it.

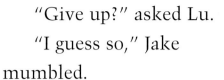

"Now, let's go," said Clancy. "There's no time to lose."

Lu and Clancy headed for the Drop of Doom. Jake swallowed hard and shuffled behind them.

Lu's Holey Card Trick

Lu and Clancy walked through a playing card. But you might want to try this with a piece of paper.

You'll need:

• a piece of writing paper • scissors

1. Fold the paper in half lengthwise and cut out a piece as shown.

2. Cut the paper along the lines shown here. Never cut right through the paper. Make 13 cuts in all.

3. Carefully unfold the paper and climb through it.

Hint: The more cuts you make, the bigger the hole. But always make an odd number of cuts.

Chapter 8

The Drop of Doom

As they got closer to the Drop of Doom, the screams of the riders grew louder. Jake's face got whiter and whiter. "Oooh," he groaned. "I think I feel a stomach ache coming on."

Finally, they arrived at the Drop of Doom. They looked up, way up. They could see the cars spin wildly, pause, then drop like a rock before swooping up again. Jake clutched his stomach.

Lu and Clancy put their heads together.

"When 'Pooches in Paradise' plays, Frank and Horace will stop the ride," said Clancy. "We have to keep them from grabbing the loot and getting away."

Lu nodded. "This could be dangerous. We'd better get Detective Doberman."

Just then, the song "Pooches in Paradise" started up. "No time," yelled Clancy.

"I'll do it," said Jakc, and he melted into the crowd.

"Let's go," shouted Lu. "You take Horace, and I'll take Frank."

Lu climbed aboard the Drop of Doom. Clancy grabbed a banana.

A banana?

Chapter 9
Stop the Drop

The wind swept through Lu's fur. All around her, riders screamed as the Drop of Doom lurched and twisted. She could hear "Pooches in Paradise" playing. Suddenly the ride screeched to a halt. The cars swung wildly back and forth. It was time for action!

Lu undid her seatbelt and crawled out of the car.
She was so high up that people on the ground looked
like ants. Taking a deep breath, she started swinging
from car to car. She calmed the frightened passengers
and borrowed their scarves, belts and necklaces.

On the ground, Frank's eyes were bulging. The veins on his neck stood out. "Horace," he shouted. "Get going. Grab the loot."

Wallets and loose change were raining down all around Horace, but he didn't move. He was watching Clancy. Actually, he was watching the banana swinging from Clancy's hand.

Frank grabbed a bag and started stuffing loot into it. He was reaching for a diamond ring, when he heard a piercing yell. The last thing Frank saw was the bottom of Lu's feet.

Horace licked his lips as Clancy peeled the banana. Amazingly, slices of banana fell off.

Clancy walked backward and Horace followed, grabbing each slice as it fell from the banana and stuffing it into his mouth. Clancy led him to Detective Doberman's police van. Frank was slouched inside. Clancy tossed in the banana. Horace leaped after it. The door clanked shut. The crowd cheered.

"That was one slippery trick," joked Lu.

"No problem. It was a slice," laughed Clancy.

"It was very ap-pealing," added Detective Doberman.

"Lu and Clancy, dog detectives, save the day again!"

Clancy's Sliced Banana Trick

Here's how Clancy sliced the banana before he peeled it.

You'll need:

- a toothpick or plastic cocktail stick • a banana

1. Push the toothpick into the banana, but not so far that it comes out the other side. Gently wiggle the toothpick from side to side.

2. Repeat this in a few places along the banana. This will slice the banana. When you peel it, slices will fall off.

Chapter 10
Ride of a Lifetime

"What a great day," sighed Lu. "What was your favorite part?"

"The look on Frank's face just before you landed on him."

Lu and Clancy laughed.

"I can think of one thing that was funnier," said Lu. "The look on Jake's face when the manager of the carnival gave us all lifetime passes to the Drop of Doom!"